P9-BIC-009

3.6

Annie's Gifts

by Angela Shelf Medearis

Illustrated by Anna Rich

To Sandra and Howard, my big sister and baby brother, with love. A.S.M.

Text copyright 1994 by Angela Shelf Medearis. Illustrations copyright 1994 by Anna Rich. All rights reserved. No part of this book may be reproduced or utilized in any form or by any means, electronic or mechanical, including photocopying, recording or by any information storage and retrieval system without permission in writing from the publisher. Inquiries should be addressed to: JUST US BOOKS, INC., 356 Glenwood Ave. East Orange, NJ 07017. www.justusbooks.com

Printed in Canada/ 10 9 8 7 6
Library of Congress Catalog Number 92-71998
ISBN: 0-940975-30-0 (hardcover) 0-94075-31-9 (paperback)

JUST US BOOKS, INC.
East Orange, New Jersey

Once there lived a family that loved music. Every morning the children, Lee, Patty, and Annie, turned on some music. The floors trembled as they stomped their feet to the loud bass beat. Soon they were moving down the street to catch the school bus.

After the children left for school, Momma would turn on the radio. Momma swayed with the sweet rhythm as she sipped her coffee.

Every night, after the children were in bed, Daddy would say, "Come on honey! Let's go once around the floor." Then he and Momma slow danced to the soulful, blues music he loved.

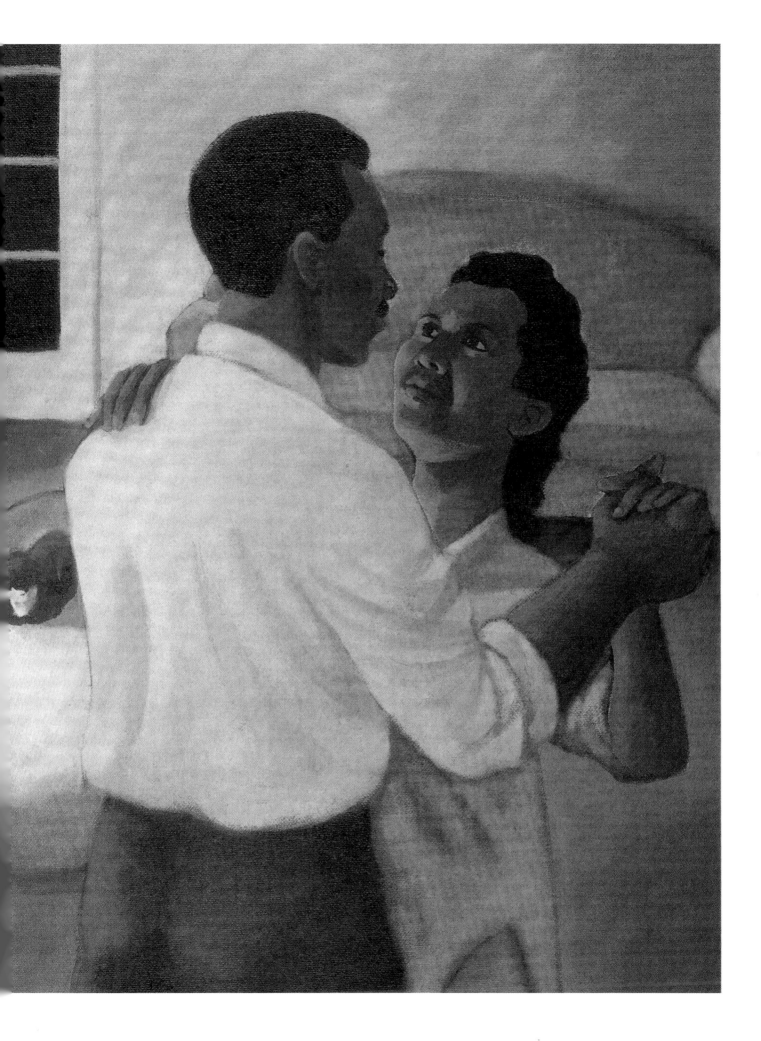

Lee loved music so much that he joined his school band. Annie thought Lee looked wonderful in his uniform with the shiny brass buttons. Lee's music sounded like the circus. When he swung into a song on the trumpet, Annie tapped her feet and clapped her hands.

Patty was a wonderful musician, too. When Patty played the piano it made Annie think of pretty colors, soft rain, and springtime flowers. Patty also had a lovely singing voice. When company came, she would entertain the guests.

"Wonderful, just wonderful," the guests would sigh and clap their hands after Patty's performance. Annie decided that she wanted to plan an instrument, too.

One day, Annie's school music teacher, Mrs. Mason, passed out instruments to the class. She gave Annie a recorder.

The class practiced a group song for months. Everyone played their part perfectly, everyone, except Annie. When Annie played, the recorder squeaked and squawked like chickens at feeding time.

"I don't think the recorder is the instrument for you," Mrs. Mason said.

"I guess you're right," Annie said, "Maybe I can play the cello."

"Let's give it a try," Mrs. Mason said. "I'll show you how to play it."

When Mrs. Mason
played the cello, it sounded
warm and carefree, like
carousel music. Annie tried
and tried, but when she
played the cello, it always
sounded like a chorus
of screeching alley cats.

"Oh," Mrs. Mason sighed
and rubbed her ears.
"Annie, darling, I just don't
think this is the instrument
for you. How would you like
to make a banner and some
posters announcing our
program?"

"Okay," said Annie. She
was disappointed, but she
did love to draw. Annie drew
while everyone else practiced.

That evening, Annie picked up Lee's trumpet and tried to play it. Her playing sounded like an elephant with a bad cold. Lee begged her to stop. Annie's feelings were hurt, but she put the trumpet away.

"I wish I could find an instrument to play," Annie told her mother.

"Cheer up!" Momma said. "We're going to get a new piano and everyone is going to take piano lessons!"

Soon, a beautiful, new piano was delivered to Annie's house. The piano was made of shiny, brown mahogany. Annie peeked under the piano lid while Patty played a song. "Melody Maker" was written in beautiful gold letters.

That week, all three children started piano lessons with Mrs. Kelly. After every lesson, Mrs. Kelly gave them new sheet music to practice.

Patty and Lee did very well. Mrs. Kelly always told them how talented they were.

Oh, but when Annie played the piano, Mrs. Kelly's smile turned into a frown. The low notes sounded like a diesel truck honking its horn, the middle ones like croaking frogs, and the high notes sobbed like a crying baby.

Once, Annie tried to sing and play the piano for her parents' guests. Her performance made everyone squirm in their chairs. Annie was so embarrassed that she went up to her room and cried. She couldn't play the recorder or the cello. She couldn't play the piano or sing or play the trumpet. Annie had never felt so sad in her life.

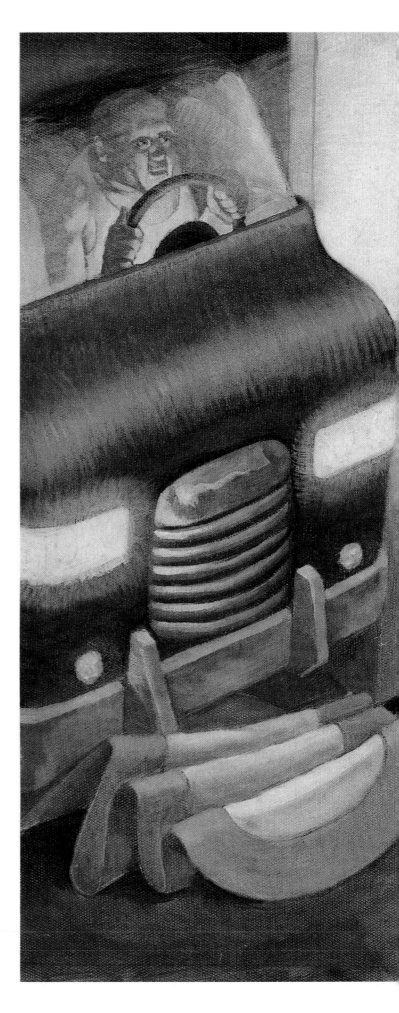

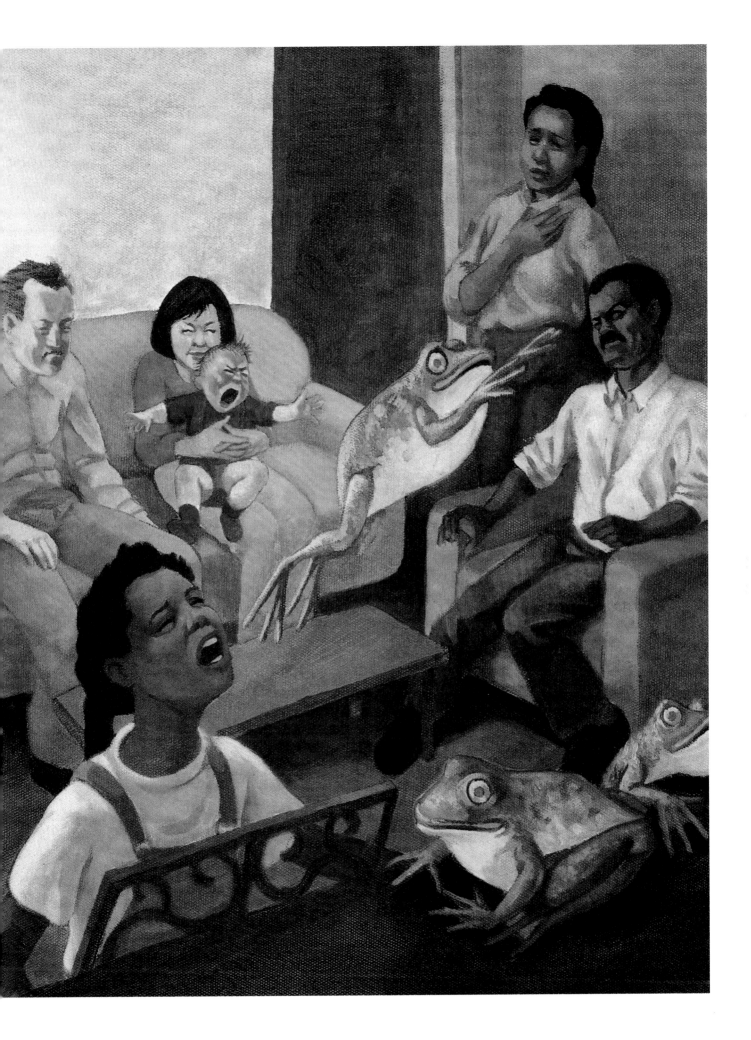

Sometimes, when Annie was sad, she liked to write poetry to make herself feel better. She decided to write a poem about music.

I love to hear music play.
I practice hard every day.
But even though I try and try,
the sounds I play
Make people laugh and cry.

That night, Annie put her poem on Daddy's pillow. Then she went to sleep.

In the morning, Daddy and Momma had a long talk with Annie.

"I just can't seem to do anything right," Annie sighed.

"Yes, you can," Daddy said. "There are lots of things you can do."

"Really, Daddy?" Annie asked.

"Of course," Momma said. "Not everyone can play the piano and sing like Patty. Not everyone can play the trumpet like Lee. That's his special gift. And not everyone can write poetry and draw beautiful pictures the way you can."

"I didn't think about it that way," Annie said. "I can't sing or play an instrument well, but I can do a *lot* of other things."

Now, if you should pass by Annie's house, you might hear Patty singing and playing on the piano. Perhaps you'll hear Lee playing his trumpet. And sometimes, if you stop and listen very, very closely, you might hear Annie playing…

her radio!

Annie plays loud, finger popping music when she feels like laughing and drawing pictures. She plays soft, sweet music when she writes her poems. She can play any kind of music she likes on her radio.

She still can't play the piano or sing like Patty, and she still can't play the trumpet like Lee.

But now Annie has found she's happiest when drawing her pictures and writing poetry. Because art and writing are Annie's gifts.

About the Author

Angela Shelf Medearis is the author of several books for children, including *Picking Peas for a Penny*, *Dancing with the Indians*, which was a "Reading Rainbow" Review Book, *The Zebra Riding Cowboy* and *Come This Far to Freedom: A History of African-Americans*. *Annie's Gifts* is based on Mrs. Medearis' childhood. She lives in Austin, Texas with her husband Michael and several stacks of children's books.

About the Illustrator

Anna Rich says her art career began in kindergarten. She much preferred coloring and drawing to her other class work. Anna Rich received her B.F.A. degree from Rhode Island School of Design and is an active member of the New York chapter of the Graphic Artists Guild. She lives in Elmont, New York with her family and cats. Anna has illustrated several picture books, including *Joshua's Masai Mask*, *Saturday at the New You*, and *Little Louis and the Jazz Band*.